# My Friendly GIANT

Written by Lauri Rubinstein

Illustrated by Mark Wayne Adams • Kurt Nestman

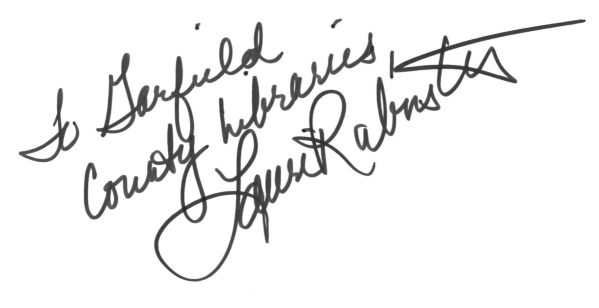

To Garfield
County libraries
Lauri Rubinstein

**Growing Field Books**
Where children go to grow!™

For information regarding permissions, contact Growing Field Books at:

**Growing Field Books**
2012 Pacific Court
Fort Collins, Colorado 80528
or through: info@growingfied.com

**Publisher's Cataloging-in-Publication**
(*Provided by Quality Books, Inc.*)

Rubinstein, Lauri.
My friendly giant / by Lauri Rubinstein;
illustrators, Mark W. Adams & Kurt W. Nestman.
p. cm.
SUMMARY: My Friendly Giant is a personal growth and leadership story that invites children to listen to their inner voice.

LCCN 2011938360
ISBN-13: 978-0-9770391-6-6
ISBN-10: 0-9770391-6-1

1. Giants--Juvenile fiction. 2. Leadership--Juvenile fiction. 3. Self-actualization (Psychology)--Juvenile fiction. [1. Giants--Fiction. 2. Leadership--Fiction. 3. Self-actualization (Psychology)--Fiction.]
I. Adams, Mark W., ill. II. Nestman, Kurt W., ill.
III. Title.

PZ7.R83136My 2012          [E]
QBI11-600196

Printed in China / January 2012

This book is dedicated to...

My two miracles,
Tanner & Taylor
*You bring me more joy than I could have ever imagined.*

My husband, Mark
*Thank you for your love and support.*

Dad and Mom
*Thank you for your belief.*

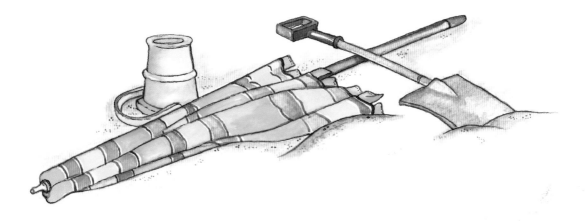

We all have a limitless friendly giant living within us.

Our giant is always there when we need it most.

2

Our giant's limitless nature within
doesn't understand "I can't."

3

It only understands "I can."

Sometimes we are told, "You can't; you are too little."

But our giant within us
knows that with a little practice and time
we can do anything.

Our giant within never lets us quit.

Because our limitless giant knows
that we are always capable of doing our best.

Sometimes at school
I don't understand things right away.

Then I hear my giant within telling me,
"Keep trying. You will get it with a little more effort."

10

But sometimes when I am trying to do something,

I get frustrated.

My giant will tell me,
"Take a deep breath
and try a new way.
You can do it."

12

I DID IT!

14

IN CASE OF EMERGENCY PULL LEVER

When I make a mistake,
my giant within tells me, "It's okay."

My giant reminds me that with every mistake comes a lesson.

Sometimes at school
other kids laugh at me and I feel sad.

But then I hear my giant within,
and I smile when he tells me,
"No matter what they say, you are loved."

My giant also tells me that what really matters
is that I love myself.

19

Because I can't control what others think
and what they say.

My giant reminds me that
no matter what is going on in my life,
I can always be happy.

Most of all, I love my giant
because he reminds me of all that I have.

And when I remember all that I have,
I feel grateful.

23

My limitless giant within is my best friend.

He encourages me to play fully, as hard as I can.
And he tells me that one day,
all of my dreams will come true.

I know they will.

Because my limitless giant within me says so!

It's my limitless nature!

28

# Lauri Rubinstein Inspires:

"Through the My Friendly Giant series, Lauri Rubinstein conveys a strong message for children and adults everywhere to listen to their inner voice and love the person they are, regardless of how the world evaluates them."

*—Shirley Oppenheimer, Sr. National Sales Director*
*Mary Kay Cosmetics*

"Here's a great read with strong, positive messages. It is a powerful book for building emotionally healthy and self-confident children!"

*—Tom Penzel, Principal*
*Carbondale Community School*

"Great authors inspire us to believe not only in what we are...but also in what we are capable of becoming.

Today that inspiration is delivered by Lauri Rubinstein, who invites all of us to listen to our magical inner voice and open the door to our unlimited life possibility. *My Friendly Giant* is a MUST READ for our youngest generation!"

*—Mark Hoog, President*
*Growing Field International*

Visit Lauri's website at **www.myfriendlygiant.com** to engage her for school visits, speaking engagements, and seminars!